T0210121

The Mysterious Bottle

Neill Jones

authorHOUSE®

AuthorHouse™
1663 Liberty Drive
Bloomington, IN 47403
www.authorhouse.com
Phone: 1 (800) 839-8640

Published by AuthorHouse 02/14/2020

ISBN: 978-1-7283-4511-6 (sc)
ISBN: 978-1-7283-4510-9 (e)

Print information available on the last page.

Any people depicted in stock imagery provided by Getty Images are models, and such images are being used for illustrative purposes only. Certain stock imagery © Getty Images.

This book is printed on acid-free paper.

Preface

Thank you for picking this book up and giving it a try.

In my career as a teacher I always had a problem with the boys reading books and writing. Returning from the Library one day, in frustration and trying not to pull my hair out, being almost grey is enough I don't want to lose my hair as well, I said to my grade, "Why don't you borrow books from the Library?"

The answer from the boys was that there wasn't anything in the Library that they wanted to read.

The discussion that followed was interesting because the boys said that no one had ever asked them what they wanted to read. The books were chosen each year by a middle aged female who I am sure was doing a fantastic job, just not choosing books that appealed to boys. So the school invited a whole lot of publishers to come to the school to show the boys the books that would appeal to them.

The school also gave me some money to buy some graphic novels/comics for the boys to read (I'm a big fan) and reading became less of a struggle. I also took in gaming magazines for the boys to read.

The stories I have written are stories that I hope will appeal to reluctant readers and also good readers who enjoy a bit of fun.

Thomas held on as tightly as he could with his fingertips curled over a rock. His body was hanging over a drop into darkness. He had stumbled into the hole trying to catch up with his friends Zac, Josh and Cameron. They had all fallen into the hole.

If only he had a torch then he could see where the others were. He yelled out the other boys' names but got no replies.

Thomas could feel the fingers of his hand start to uncurl. Not being able to hold on any longer he lost his grip and felt himself falling, falling...

Thomas was bouncing a ball against a wall at his house trying to catch the ball with his opposite hand. He was wondering what his friend Zac was doing.

Zac was sitting in his bedroom with his X-Box controller in his hands wondering what his friend Josh was doing.

Josh was in the backyard kicking his football in the air and running to mark it before it hit the ground. He was wondering what his friend Cameron was doing.

Cameron was at home reading a book. (What do you mean boys don't read books!) He had just finished a chapter and was wondering what his friend Thomas was doing.

Thomas walked inside to find his Dad. He was going to use his Dad's phone to call Zac. It was a sore point him not having his own phone. He thought he was old enough and responsible enough to own his own phone but his Dad had told him he wasn't old enough yet.

He found his Dad vacuuming the floor and yelled really loudly because his Dad had earphones on and was listening to music at the same time.

"Dad…Dad…DAD!"

Then he stood in front of his Dad so he could see him.

Thomas' Dad turned off the vacuum cleaner and took off his earphones.

Thomas said, "Can I use the phone please, I want to ring Zac."

Thomas' Dad said, "Sure, but first I want you to answer a question. How do you get down from an elephant?"

Thomas thought for a bit and said, "Carefully?"

Thomas' Dad laughed and said, "You don't get down from an elephant, you get down from a duck."

Thomas groaned to himself. It was a Dad joke. There is nothing on Earth worse than a Dad joke. Or maybe a Dad quote. But he wanted to use the phone so he laughed politely and held out his hand. "Phone please."

He rang Zac and started talking to him but realized that Zac wasn't paying attention.

"Zac, turn off the game," Thomas said.

Zac protested, "But I am on Level 27, I only have 73 levels to go."

Thomas tried again, "Zac, pause the game and turn off the T.V. so I know that I have your full attention."

Zac grumbled but did what Thomas asked.

Thomas said, "I have to get out of the house soon. Dad is about to ask me to help with the cleaning. Let's call Josh and Cameron and we can meet at the big tree before the hills and we can do some exploring."

Zac said that he would call Josh and Cameron and they arranged a time for them all to meet.

Thomas handed the phone to his Dad and headed for the door saying he was going to do some exploring with his mates.

Thomas' Dad mentioned something about needing a hand to clean the bathroom but Thomas was already out the door and running to the meeting place.

He met up with his mates Zac, Cameron and Josh and they talked about what they would like to do.

Thomas told them about his dad teaching him to skip stones over water so they could go to the creek and he could show them how to do it.

Josh suggested going up into the hills. He thought he had seen the outline of a cave behind the trees.

Cameron and Zac shook their heads. They said that they had seen the cave too but they didn't like the look of it.

Josh asked, "Are you scared?"

Cameron and Zac looked at each other and turned back to Josh and said, "Maybe."

Josh asked, "I know. Where do our parents tell us that we are absolutely not ever allowed to go?"

Cameron replied, "Over the creek, through the trees and past the hills to the old mines."

Josh said, "Exactly, let's go."

Thomas thought for a bit and said, "I'm not sure it's a good idea."

But Cameron was being enthusiastic. "Yes, you're right, it isn't a good idea, it's a great idea. We might find some gold, we might be very rich."

As they were walking Thomas asked his friends, "How do you get down from an elephant?"

Josh said, "You would…"

Then he stopped walking. He said, "Is this something from your Dad?"

Thomas nodded.

Josh said to Thomas, "Please don't tell me the joke. It will be really, really bad. I have to keep my Dad away from your Dad or I will be hearing Dad jokes too."

Thomas thought about defending his Dad by saying that the jokes weren't all that bad but then he realized that they probably were.

Then the boys all started to talk about all of the things that they would buy with each suggestion being bigger and better than the last suggestion. Without realizing it little by little they passed the boundary they were not allowed to go past.

Soon the boys found themselves standing in front of a fence with a sign on it. It was an old sign, which had a skull and crossbones on it and in big letters said, Warning-Dangerous Area. Risk of falling into mine shafts.

Thomas said, "This is it, once we go over the fence we will have ignored our parent's boundary of where we can and can't play. Are we all sure this is what we want to do?"

The boys all said, "Yes, this is where we find our fortune," and they climbed over the wire fence and started to explore the ground that they were walking on. They made sure to walk carefully past the mines that they found.

They looked into one of the mines and thought that it went a long, long way down.

Zac said, "I will spit into the mine and we can count how long it takes to hit the bottom."

Cameron said, "But…"

Zac sucked up a gob of spit and spat it down the mine. At least that's what he tried to do. The wind picked up his spit and dropped it onto his shoe.

"Argh, not my new Nike's," he said.

Cameron said, "But Zac, you are supposed to drop a stone down the mine, not spit down it."

So Josh walked off to find a big stone. He walked it back and held it over the mineshaft. He said, "Ready to start counting? Oh wait, not you Zac because if it is over 10 you will have to take off your shoes and socks."

Zac fired back, "That's not fair. I have a condition called Dyscalculia. It means I have trouble with maths concepts like counting."

Thomas shrugged and said, "So it's true, you really do learn something new each day. Cameron, you count, you are the best at maths."

So Josh dropped the rock and Cameron counted up to 50 before it hit the bottom. Then the boys moved slowly away from the mineshaft because the rock had fallen a long, long way down.

Thomas said, "Maybe we can find a mine that is built on the side of a hill. You know, one that we can walk into."

So the boys walked down the side of a hill and followed a path through some trees.

As they walked past a raspberry bush that had grown wild Zac pointed and said, "Look over there."

Hidden by the bush was the entrance to a mine. The boys very carefully pulled some of the bush out of the way and made sure they brushed away some of the cobwebs that were in the way.

Josh asked, "What are we looking for?

Cameron replied, "Fortune and glory kid. Fortune and glory."

Thomas said, "Ah, a movie quote from my famous uncle."

Zac said, "You do not have a famous uncle, what's his name?"

Thomas smiled and said, "Uncle Indiana."

Zac laughed and said, "You do not have an uncle called Indiana Jones."

Thomas said, "Maybe I do, but maybe I don't. Next time he visits I will invite you around."

Zac stopped in the middle of the mine entrance with his mouth open, not sure if Thomas was joking or not.

Cameron bumped into him and said, "It's a movie quote Zac. Movie quote. From a fictional character."

Zac started walking again and yelled after Thomas, "I knew you were joking."

They could see a bit inside the mine but after that it started to get dark.

The boys walked further into the mine with some of them using a torch app on their phones to see where they were going.

They heard some thumping ahead of them.

They strained their eyes to see what was making the noise.

At the last moment Thomas yelled, "It's the flapping of wings. Get down."

First Thomas, then Zac, Josh and finally Cameron all dived to the ground as a cloud of bats flew over their heads.

Zac stood up brushing the dirt off him saying, "What's the big deal? They are only bats."

Josh said, "You mean the bats that can give you rabies."

Zac said, "Oh right, stay away from bats."

Cameron said, "I read where some snakes had learned to work together and hunt bats as they fly out of a cave."

The boys looked at the ground that they were standing on. None of them liked snakes.

Thomas said, "Not helping Cameron."

The boys wandered further into the mine.

Josh asked, "What do you think we will find, Gold? Diamonds? Rubies? Kryptonite?"

Zac said, "Kryptonite, the only thing I am scared of, it takes away my super powers."

The other boys fell to the ground laughing loudly about that.

Thomas said, "You are scared of falling off your bike."

Josh said, "You don't like it when you have to stay inside and finish off your school work during lunch time."

Cameron added, "I thought you told me you were afraid of something in your wardrobe."

Zac thought for a bit and said, "Okay, all of those things and Kryptonite. And don't ever joke about the wardrobe, that's a really scary place. I have told you about my wardrobe monster but every time I invite you over to look at it you all say no."

Thomas said, "My Dad told me that he read about explorers that try to go as deep into the

Earth as they possibly can. Spelunkers he called them. The deepest anyone has gone is just over 2 kilometres. He also told me that the explorers sometimes wedge themselves in so tight that they use their fingers to shift dirt to move them forward.

Then Thomas took a big breath in and slowly let it out. He thought to himself, I am not claustrophobic.

Josh stopped walking and said, "Right, I think that's enough exploring. It's time to go home while we can still stand up in this mine."

Cameron said, "But we haven't found our fortune yet, just half an hour more."

The boys checked the time on their phones and agreed that they could spend another 30 minutes exploring before they had to head home.

Thomas realized that his shoelace was undone so he called out to the others, "Wait, I have to tie up my shoelace."

The other boys called out, "You can catch up."

Thomas hurried because he had no phone or light. He finished tying his shoelace and heard the boys yell out in front of him. He thought they called out... 'hole' and then the cave went dark. He stumbled forward and felt himself falling into a hole. Thomas twisted around and held on as tightly as he could with his fingers curled onto some rocks at the edge of the hole. His body was hanging over the edge of a drop into darkness.

Thomas could feel the fingers of his hand start to uncurl. He lost his grip and felt himself falling, falling…

For about three feet.

Then his mates caught him.

It was just a short drop into the hole.

His mates thought it was funny.

Thomas, who thought he was going to die, was swearing (words which we cannot repeat here)

Zac covered his ears saying, "My goodness Thomas, my delicate ears cannot hear such words."

Thomas yelled, "I thought I was going to die. Why didn't you you say that the hole wasn't that deep?"

Cameron shrugged, "We knew you were safe. We thought it would be funny."

Thomas started to tear up, "I thought you were all dead. I thought I had lost all of my mates."

The other boys took a sudden interest in their shoes.

Zac apologized. "I know we play jokes on each other all of the time. This probably wasn't a good time for a joke."

He put his arm around Thomas' shoulder and said, "On behalf of us all I don't think that we should play any jokes on each other that involve any of us being in danger."

Josh and Thomas agreed with Zac but Cameron paused and said, "Unless it is really, really funny."

The other boys said, "No, no jokes about danger," but they couldn't get Cameron to agree. They realized that somewhere in one of their adventures Cameron intended to play a trick on them probably when the boys were in a scary situation.

So the boys looked at the hole that they had fallen into and searched for a way to get out. They talked about holes in the rocks that they could use for hand or footholds. As they started to climb out Cameron noticed what looked like a piece of glass sticking out of the dirt.

He said, "Hang on guys, I think I have found something."

Thomas called down, "Do you need a hand?"

Cameron replied, "Nope, I'm good, just give me a minute."

He cleared away some dirt until the bottle's spout was sticking out. He pulled on the bottle but it wasn't coming out as easy as he thought it would. It was almost as if the bottle was meant to stay there. With one last effort the bottle popped out of the wall.

Cameron used the torch on his phone to look at the bottle. It was an unusual shape. It looked green in colour and he remembered his grandfather showing him an old ginger beer bottle with a glass stopper inside it. He shook the bottle and heard it rattle. He looked inside the bottle but couldn't quite see what was inside. Was that a …

He jumped in fright as Zac yelled down the hole, "Hurry up Cameron, our 30 minutes is almost up."

He threw the bottle up to the boys saying, "Look what I found."

After he had climbed out of the hole the boys walked back out of the cave being careful to watch out for bats from above their heads and snakes beneath their feet.

They blinked and squinted their eyes shut as they walked into the bright sunshine. Then they wandered back along the track until they had stepped over the fence and past the warning sign.

Thomas said, "Okay we are officially back in the 'safe zone' but we can't tell our parents where we have been or we will be grounded and our life will be home, school and home again. Probably for a long time, I don't want to do that."

The other boys nodded their heads in agreement.

When they found a spot to sit in the shade of some trees the boys sat on the ground and looked at the bottle that Cameron had found.

Zac laughed and said, "So our fortune is not gold or diamonds…"

Josh added, "Or Kryptonite"

…but a glass bottle. Doesn't quite pay for a pool in my backyard and a slide from my roof into the pool."

The boys handed the bottle backwards and forwards trying to work out why someone would put the bottle into the mine.

Cameron said, "I think that there is something inside the bottle." He picked up a stick and moved the glass stopper in the bottle.

They watched as smoke came out of the bottle and 'BLAM' the boys were knocked backwards onto the ground as the air from the bottle turned slowly from smoke into the shape of a man.

He shouted, "I am free! At last, after hundreds of years stuck in the bottle, I AM FREE."

The boys looked on in amazement as the man stood up tall and straight. He wore mismatched clothing. On his head he wore a top hat. He wore a jacket with a rainbow bow tie. He also wore a kilt with long socks and Doc Martens boots.

He saw the boy's expressions and said, "I had to keep myself amused somehow." Then he clicked his fingers and his clothing changed to look like what the boys were wearing, shorts, t-shirt and runners.

"Nice magic trick, well done," said Josh

The man said, "Magic? A magic trick you say. Okay, we will call it magic if you like."

He then said, "I am sorry, where are my manners, my name is Mr. Djinn and your names?"

Zac said, "I'm Zac and these are my friends, Thomas, Josh and Cameron."

Mr. Djinn said, "Thank you for freeing me boys, your reward for releasing me is 3 wishes that I will make come true. But I caution you to use them wisely. Once you make your wish you can't take it back. So think very carefully about what you want"

The boys all started talking at once

Thomas called out, "Everyone stop. Think of a question each."

So they sat quietly for a few minutes.

Josh asked the first question, "Can we ask for more than 3 wishes?"

Mr. Djinn said, "No, you only get 3 wishes."

Zac asked, "Will our wishes come true?"

Mr. Djinn said, "Yes, you're wishes will come true."

Cameron asked, "How do we get our wishes?"

Mr. Djinn replied, "You say to me, I wish for…"

Thomas thought for a moment more and he asked, "Is there a trick to your wishes?"

Mr. Djinn smiled broadly, bowed and said, "Your wish is my command."

Thomas looked at the other boys and said, "It's an answer, but not a direct answer."

He looked at Mr. Djinn and said, "No offence."

Mr. Djinn smiled again and said, "None taken."

But Thomas didn't think that the smile quite reached Mr. Djinn's eyes.

Josh laughed and said, "It looks as if we have found our fortune after all."

The boys went into a huddle and whispered amongst themselves about what they were going to wish for first. They decided not to be greedy and that they would wish for one million dollars divided between the four of them.

Mr. Djinn asked, "Do you have your first wish?"

He pointed at Cameron and said, "That boy who found the bottle gets to ask the wishes. It is something to do with the genie book of rules and regulations"

Cameron said, "I wish for…

Thomas yelled, "Stop, wait. Do you remember our maths class on weight? One million dollars in $1 notes would weigh 1 ton, we can't carry that."

Mr. Djinn flashed a look of disappointment but quickly smiled again.

Cameron started again, "I wish for one million dollars to be shared equally between the four of us with the money to be paid into our bank accounts."

Mr. Djinn clicked his fingers and said, "It is done, call me when you are ready for your next wish," and he disappeared back into his bottle in a puff of smoke.

Cameron picked up the bottle and the boys started walking back home. Josh was smiling because he had used an app on his phone to check his bank balance and he now had two hundred and fifty thousand and ten dollars in his bank account.

The boys were all smiling now because they would have money in their bank accounts as well.

All of a sudden they realized that they were going to have to explain to their parents how they got all of their money.

Cameron said, "Surely we can be forgiven for walking outside our boundary if we can show our parents all of the money we now have and I guess we will have to share some of it. Or most of it."

Halfway home the boys noticed huge black clouds forming in the skies behind them. They started to move a bit quicker towards home

Suddenly it started to rain with hailstones the size of golf balls so the boys started running but were knocked off their feet by a huge wind that swept past them on its way into town.

The boys picked themselves up and started running towards home as fast as they could only slowing down when Zac fell behind.

They could hear the sounds of sirens, as they got closer to their homes.

When they got to Thomas' house, his Dad was standing out the front of a partially destroyed house.

He said, "Oh boys, thank goodness you are okay. Your parents and I were so worried about you with this horrible weather and you being stuck outside in it."

Thomas gave his Dad a hug and asked him if he was okay.

He said he was and added, "The strangest thing happened. Zac, Josh and Cameron's houses are like ours. The storm and fierce wind hit only our houses. No one else in town had their house damaged. The insurance companies think it will cost about a quarter of a million dollars to repair each of the houses. We don't know where we are going to find the money."

From the bottle, they thought that they could hear laughter.

The boys were a bit frustrated and angry. Josh said, "That's okay, we know where we can find the money."

When all of the parents were together, Cameron put the bottle on a table that had been blown outside and he told them where they had found the bottle and what had happened.

He said, "We get 3 wishes and our first wish was for some money."

Josh said, "I was going to buy a pool for the back yard with a slide from the roof into the pool."

Cameron said, "With my money, I was going to send my parents away on a holiday"

Thomas said, "It was nice knowing that we had some money in the bank to use if we needed it."

Zac said, "I was going to buy a new wardrobe… one without a monster in it. Oh and give the rest to my parents."

The parents were relieved that they had the money to pay for the houses but they were not happy to know where the boys had been exploring.

Being grounded were words that the boys heard a lot of.

Thomas hoped his Dad was joking about him being grounded until his 25th birthday.

Zac, Josh, Thomas and Cameron promised not to make any more wishes without speaking to their parents first.

The next few days were pretty normal except for the work being done on the boy's houses and the fact that none of the boys had any free time because their parents had given them lots of work to do.

Zac was shocked when his parents took away his X-Box system.

"But, but, what will I do?" he asked.

When he was told that he could read a book he fell back onto his bed and complained about being punished twice.

As Thomas was walking past the T.V. carrying the rubbish to the bin, he heard the news reporter talking about a crisis between North Korea and America and the possibility that nuclear weapons might be used.

He had the beginning of an idea and asked his Dad if he could have a meeting with his friends and their parents.

The parents sat down and had a glass of water while the boys sat and talked through Thomas' idea. He had suggested using a wish to destroy all of the nuclear weapons.

They talked to the parents about their idea.

With this wish we can make our planet a safer place for everyone. No one need live in fear of being attacked just because they were different from the people who lived in the country next to theirs.

Josh said, "No more wars between countries."

Zac said, "No more innocent people being shot."

Cameron said, "We could also get rid of all of the biological weapons as well."

The boys put their heads together and thought about the types of weapons that they could get rid of. Eventually they suggested that they get rid of all types of weapons.

Cameron's Dad said, "What about baseball bats?"

Cameron said, "No, Dad, a baseball bat isn't a weapon."

Thomas' Dad said, "But it could be. What about the bread knife I use to slice the toast?"

Thomas said, No, that's not a weapon, we just mean all the big weapons, the ones that can kill a lot of people at the same time."

Finally with all of the parents and the boys in agreement about what weapons of mass destruction were, Cameron flicked the stopper and out came Mr. Djinn. He greeted the parents and asked the boys what their next wish would be.

Zac said, "No tricks this time."

But Mr. Djinn just smiled and asked Cameron to make his wish.

Cameron said, "I wish for all of the weapons of mass destruction on Earth to be destroyed so that our planet and all of our people can live in peace."

Mr. Djinn clicked his fingers and again disappeared back into his bottle.

The next morning the boys and their parents sat down in front of their T.V. to see what was going to happen.

The boys waited to see if they were to be tricked again. They kept their fingers crossed hoping that this time they would get their wish right and Mr

Djinn couldn't do something to spoil their careful thinking.

All the people on the planet were pleasantly surprised when the United Nations and all of its 193 nations extended hands in friendship and destroyed all of their weapons. To the cheers of people all around the world, the United Nation's leader said that everyone could look forward to a future of peace.

With the weapons all destroyed by all of the countries on the planet the boys gave themselves high fives. Their parents were so pleased that they decided that the boys consequence of being 'grounded would finish immediately. Zac even got his X-Box back.

One week later, the alien space ships arrived.

The message that the aliens sent was that all of the people on the planet were to be transported back to the Alien home planet as slaves. After arrival the people from planet Earth were expected to dig in mines for precious metals.

The United Nations Secretary General sadly told all of the people on the planet they could not be protected because all the weapons of mass destruction had been destroyed, and there was nothing left to fight the Aliens with. Planet Earth was not prepared for the invasion.

He told all of the people on Earth to spend as much time with their families as they could.

The boys were all around at Thomas' place watching it on their T.V.

Zac kicked the ginger beer bottle as hard as he could, but all that achieved was Zac getting a sore toe.

"Tricked again, moaned Josh. We have to make a choice, send away the aliens and hope that no more aliens come or get all our weapons back and fight them."

Cameron said, "I have been reading up on our Mr. Djinn. If we use our last wish, we will be letting the genie out of the bottle. He would be free to rule over us all and there would be nothing or no one powerful enough to stop him. He would be unbeatable"

They heard loud sinister snickering from the bottle.

Thomas said, "I wish we had more wishes."

Cameron reminded him that the genie had only given us three wishes. He said, "Maybe we could have wished for more wishes. After all, we just took his word for it and he hasn't been very honest."

Josh wondered, "What if we wished for the bottle and everything in it to be destroyed?"

"Or, we could wish for the stopper in the bottle to be permanently glued in place so Mr. Djinn could never get out of the bottle again," said Cameron.

Now the boys were talking excitedly about what they could do with the last wish. Zac and Thomas suggested that they use the last wish to take away his powers so that he would be a slave like the humans.

The laughter from inside the bottle suddenly stopped. Now there was a knocking sound coming from inside the bottle.

"Or, said Zac, we could wish for the genie to turn himself into a statue. After all, he did say, your wish is my command."

Josh laughed and said, "We could write something about it. In fact I have the perfect suggestion for what we could write on a plaque to put in front of the statue."

Please feel free

To have a pee

For good fortune and money

Nice food and honey

On this stone you see

Thomas gave Josh a fist bump. "Paying attention when we were learning limericks in class. Nice job."

The genie could stand it no longer. He forced his way past the stopper and the boys watched in amusement as the bottle spun around in circles and Mr Djinn exited the bottle a bit dazed and dizzy.

Mr. Djinn stood to his full height, red faced with anger and thundered, "You would not dare!" Cameron laughed and said, "Dude, we are four young boys who sit around and laugh at who farts the loudest. Of course we would dare."

Thomas said, "We only have one more wish left. Get the aliens to leave, get back all of the weapons or turn you into a statue. I'm not sure of what the other boys are thinking but I'm voting with our last wish to turn you into a statue."

Thomas looked at Josh and Zac who both said, "Statue."

Cameron said, "Okay, statue it is. I wish for Mr. Djinn to…"

"Wait!" shouted Mr. Djinn.

Zac said, "Of course, how foolish we have been. We can't turn you into a statue without knowing what colour statue you would like to be."

Mr. Djinn said, "No, no, no. No statue, no plaque and definitely no pee."

Cameron said, "But we only have one wish left."

Mr. Djinn's shoulders dropped. He said, "I may have a solution."

He turned to Cameron and said," You could use your last wish to take you back to where you found me. Your houses will be repaired; there will be no alien space ships and your countries will get all of their weapons back.

I will be back in my bottle and you will be in the hole in the cave and you won't pull the bottle out of the dirt."

Zac said, "Or we could turn you into a stone statue with Josh's great limerick written on it."

Mr. Djinn said, "Please don't…"

Thomas said, "How do we know that this isn't just another horrible trick you are going to play on us?"

Mr. Djinn pleaded again, "Please don't…"

Cameron said, "I wish for all of the things that you said to happen."

Mr. Djinn clicked his fingers and the boys found themselves standing in the hole in the cave and Cameron was holding the bottle with Mr. Djinn standing in front of the bottle.

Mr. Djinn said, "Your houses are repaired, your planets' weapons are back and there are no more aliens."

Cameron said, "And you are back in the bottle," and quickly pushed the stopper in behind the genie and the bottle back into the dirt.

The boys climbed out of the hole and made their way out of the mine. They pulled the raspberry bushes across the entrance.

Thomas said, "I hope that no one else finds the bottle for a very long time."

As they headed back home, Josh said, "That was a great adventure, no fortune, but better than watching T.V."

Cameron said, "Sure, we could have all been turned into slaves for aliens…or used as a food product." He shivered.

Zac said, "At one stage we did have a quarter of a million dollars, at least for a few minutes."

He thought for a bit and said, "We should have a name for our group. Maybe we could be The Fantastic Four."

Thomas said, "Um, no, I'm pretty sure that name is trademarked by Marvel."

Cameron said, "How about The Famous Four?"

Thomas said, "Probably too close to The Enid Blyton characters."

Zac said, "Who are they?'

Thomas started to say, "They're from a book…" but Zac had lost interest because it involved reading.

Thomas said, "How about we call ourselves The Fearless Four."

The boys tried it out...'The Fearless Four'... and they liked the sound of it.

As they continued to walk home Thomas asked aloud, "I wonder what other kind of adventures The Fearless Four will have?"

Zac looked at the book Thomas was holding in his hands. He asked if it was the book about The Mysterious Bottle

Thomas said, "Yes, it is our first story but I have put in some pictures of what we looked like in some of our other adventures. That is what we look like on the back cover."

"Other adventures?" Cameron asked

Josh asked, "Where did you get that photo of me standing with the cricket bat?

Thomas said that in one adventure they get hold of a portal gun they use to jump in and out of adventures. I took some photos of some of the things that we did.

The other boys jumped on Thomas demanding to know what had happened in the other Fearless Four adventures but Thomas could only tell them where the pictures came from, he said as soon as the portal gun disappeared then so did his memory of what had happened on their adventure.

The boys all punched Thomas on the arm.

"Ow, said Thomas, What was that for?"

Cameron said, "If we are a team, then we work together, we don't go off by ourselves and we stick together."

Josh and Zac both nodded.

Thomas said, "You are right, we, need to stay together to and look after each other. Now who wants to see their picture?"

The first picture is of me and I am looking pretty heroic which is my normal self in most of out stories…I hope."

The other boys snorted with laughter.

Thomas protested, "I can be heroic. This is a picture of me when we Battle Shadows."

Thomas put down a picture of Josh who was standing with a cricket bat.

He said, "I am pretty sure I can guess this one, we are playing a game of cricket."

Thomas said, "Yes, but I can't remember who we played against."

Cameron said, "I am looking pretty happy in my picture, what have we just done?"

Thomas said, "I can't remember, I seem to think it had something to do with learning a lesson."

Zac protested, "But I look like I am scared. Where is my toughness and my courage?"

The other boys shrugged their shoulders and Thomas said, "But this is the story of where you meet your wardrobe monster."

You were pretty scared, but of course we all were, with that nasty claw coming out of the cupboard."

Josh said, "I'm sure there will be other pictures of you in some of the other stories where you will be braver. After all, you were the one who said we were The Fearless Four and not the Timid Three."

As for you dear reader, you will have to use your imagination as to what you think The Fearless Four look like.

(Or wait until the next book!)

Afterward

This is where I thank the people who have played a huge role in me being able to write my stories. Without their support these stories would just be whirling around in my head trying to get out.

My wife Lynn, who always encourages me to write my ideas down. I would sit and watch T.V. with a notebook by my side and a pencil to write bits and pieces to make my story complete. She also feeds me, which is good because I have a lifetime ban in the kitchen (but that's another story)

She is always positive and supportive and reads my stories to check for spelling mistakes and to see how the story flows and I thank her for that.

My sister Elinor for her faith in my writing. Thank you for using all of your educational experience and knowledge in making sure the stories appealed to a wide range of readers. Thank you also for your fantastic blurb you helped write to showcase the stories as books that can be read by boys who enjoy reading as well as for boys who are reluctant readers.

My daughter Aimee, who sometimes makes suggestions to improve the stories, and help make them better. Her confidence in my writing means that I can take some risks or try some things that I normally wouldn't.

My son Thomas who is a part of The Fearless Four. Without you, there would be no stories as I think about some of the stories that I would tell you just before you went to sleep. Now I have the opportunity to write the stories down and share with the readers some of the stories that you and your mates got up to. I can turn these stories into a book and share your stories with other children who enjoy reading or enjoy having stories read to you.

Thank you to you, the person who has picked up this book to give it a try, I hope you enjoy it and the other Fearless Four stories to follow.

Printed in the United States
By Bookmasters